WE WERE DOLPHINS TOGETHER

WE

WERE

DOLPHINS

TOGETHER

Dedicated to the Pacific Ocean

and to every girl I've ever loved

<3

"Mother I never knew,

every time I see the ocean,

every time —"

Kobayashi Issa

"I have the best advice for women[...]
Get your fuckin' ass up and work. It
seems like nobody wants to work
these days."

- Kim Kardashian

WELCOME TO QUIZNOS

Jake had been giving me rides to work at the sandwich shop.

"Say that again" he whispered to me in my apartment complex's Easter yellow elevator. His eyes jetted across me as he tugged at my work visor, almost brotherly, front teeth pressing the cush of his bottom lip to show me how madly he meant it.
"Make me" I whimpered, a puppy with breasts. He slammed me into the wall so hard the elevator jumped. Then his cock jumped. I felt it tensing. I yanked him down by his long lobe and licked his ear slowly, root to tip. I breathed into it, damp and hot, and I told him what he wanted to hear.

"Welcome to Quiznos".

He groaned and kissed me...

WANT!

Another suicide adjacent text from Fernando today. "I love you all so much. This doesn't mean I'm weak. I'm just the worst kind of gay man in LA." My friend Fernando always threatens suicide when he doesn't get what he wants. Poor Fernando. He is not self aware enough to know that not getting what he wants IS what he wants. He has a heart that wants to want and it's hard to predict what a heart like that will latch onto.
Fernando's heart wants to be lovelorn. His feelings toward a lover are one thousand percent "eh" until the lover leaves, and once he does, Fernando gets 51/50'd, arrested, or at mildest, sets up a group chat with me, his mom, and 5 of his exes and pens a vaguely suicidal text that sends everyone except for me into upheaval. I send a gif of Gordon Ramsey rolling his eyes.
"Why not just say nothing? You dumb heartless bitch" His sister responds to me. 4 people heart her message.

I understand Fernando because I too have a wanter's heart, but mine wants this feeling, maybe it's a memory, of an Encino summer night at 16, swimming in nothing but Jake's Lil Wayne tour tee, watching the hot white pool light seep through the cotton, my born saggy breasts bobbing gracefully, the seaweed sway of wet auburn hair, eternally seraphic.

I've always had a holy relationship with water although my first memory of it is sad and embarrassing. I was thirsty. I was 3. My babysitter Meriam suggested "agua". She had been teaching me Spanish, but the word "agua" was yet to stick, so I was excited to try a new and exciting flavor. When aqua turned out to be fucking water, clear cold nothingness, I was devoured by a sharp disappointment, the kind that equals nap. I awoke at sunset to my mother smiling down on me. "Did someone have a water meltdown?" she asked. My mom told me I didn't cry at all when I was born. I just gawked around the

room, breathing it all in. My theory is that I was already looking something to want. A dream. A passion. A boyfriend. She used to say I went "dolphin mode" in the ocean, and she said when I was swimming was the only time I wasn't trying to get somewhere else. I am athletic by zero means, but I am an extremely fast swimmer. In Italy last year, I swam in an ancient Grecian trading port.
"Conosci quest'acqua!" a saggy Italian man shouted to me from a rock.
"What!"
"You know this water!"

I was having panic attacks every waking hour last year, which was not as bad as it sounds because I was only awake about 9 hours per day. I slept all the time because panic attacks are exhausting, and because my dreams were usually flying ones where I was a giant seagull soaring around, fucking everyone. This was, as you can imagine, much more fun than sobbing and shaking every time I left the house, as had become my waking normal. As far as I was concerned, every doorknob, every car handle, every floor and every surface were covered in LSD, and if I touched anything I would end up in the insane asylum, or I would lose control, commit murder, and spend the rest of my life in prison.

I thought a vacation might make me feel better, but I spent all day in my Cancun hotel room. On the 5th day, I worked up the courage to go for a snorkel. An angel fish scuttled behind a rock, and for a moment there was true, true peace. Fernando blames his father for the hole in his heart. He reads me an email his father sent him that is comically villainous.

"You think sucking all these men's dicks is going to get you to heaven! HA! Wrong! Be real my son. I have always been ashamed of you. Your aunts and uncles are ashamed of you. You are a great disgrace in my life."

I understand daddy issues. I think about my father and my chest aches. What's the closest we've ever been to touching without knowing it? Have we sat in the same seat at the movies, drank from the

same glass, opened the same door?
Have we said "I love you" to different
people at the exact same moment but
known in the cockles of our heart that
we meant it for each other? Sometimes
when I'm lonely I pretend he's watching
me. He's next to me at the red light. Did
he see me across a hotel lobby once?
Did he hear my shoes clacking on the
marble, arms flung over a lover? Did he
smile? Did he cry? Could he have sworn
I saw him? Did he duck behind a pillar?
Or maybe he's been watching me at a
time I wish he hadn't been. Has he
watched me pacing the streets with an
ice pack on my neck mid panic attack or
at 3 am in a CVS parking lot ripping the
sensor off a stolen package of Plan B
with my teeth?
And does he Google my name the way I
do his? And when he does, is he
ashamed to find me with a credit score
in the 400s and an Instagram where I
frequently flaunt my bare tuchus? Does
my body relieve him of some kind of
guilt? Maybe he imagines me tiny and
helpless and then finds me thick and
sturdy and thanks God he hasn't

abandoned someone who needs his protection. Or is there catharsis in the fact that I haven't changed my last name, the piece of him I sign on every dotted line?

These are all questions I don't want answered. I want to WANT the questions answered, and there's a huge difference. The romance exists because knowing is impossible. The questions are, to me, waves crashing. They are whale songs. The questions are lullabies. They settle me. I couldn't sleep without them. I Google photo after photo of my father and I'm flooded with the joy and terror of searching for God in his iris. If I squint I swear I can see Him, big and bright like the moon.

The other night I pulled over on PCH to a full moon and sat on the shore, milking a moment, singing Moon River to the sky and pretending to be the center of the universe. But the ocean humbled me, the way it does, and with a slap and a hiss seeped into my tennis shoes before I could scramble away.

I love the water. Anyone who knows me knows I love the water. I love the pools and the baths and the oceans and the rivers and the lakes and the puddles of this world. And I know the water will never love me back. Not me specifically. That's part of why I love the water so much, because it loves us all the same. But still I want the water to want me and because I want the impossible I will always have a want to fall back on if in case, God forbid, everything else I want comes true.

Maybe a want that large could settle Fernando, I suggest over the phone. "I just WANT to be happy" Fernando weeps. He is trashed off a handle of New Amsterdam vodka at 11 AM on a Wednesday, blasting Peggy Lee and teaching his parakeet to whistle. "Why can't I be happy?" "Shut up, Fernando. You are happy." A long pause. Finally, a laugh breaks his sobs.

"Bitch, you're so right." I pick him up and we go shopping.

CLEO

Cleo met some ginger meth addict at her Rancho Cucamonga rehab and married him after knowing him for 3 days. I was not surprised. Cleo had a knack for sniffing out the smelliest turd in every room and falling in love with it. I think she liked how gorgeous she felt in the beady eyes of hideous losers, even though she was gorgeous to everyone, especially me.

I was better at hiding our problem than Cleo was. Cleo's frail body could not harbor the 7 Xanax bars we were both housing daily like my tree trunk body could. I worked at Urban Outfitters, and when I wasn't stealing salads off the mobile order pickup rack at the Sweetgreen next door, I was a gregarious and chipper sales associate. Meanwhile, Cleo spent her days with crusted beans on her lips in a 3XL hoodie that fit her like a dress, sleeping in movie theaters and losing her purse. The power of us permeated everything I did; it was the only thing that gave me promise, made me special. Cleo had no phone privileges in rehab in an attempt to to rehabilitate her relationship with nature along with everything else. They weren't allowed to have phones, but they were allowed to marry each other.

Now that she was married she could end up anywhere. "The plan is for me to stop my birth control in the next 3 months and have a baby in the next year." She told me on our weekly allotted call. His family was from Tucson so it would probably be best to raise the baby there. Or in Hawaii. Or in Vegas.

I met Cleo when I was 14 and she was 16. She had hair like fusilli and baby green eyes and scars on her arms. The scars were fat and deep and raised. I tried to cut myself once because it seemed like a rite of passage, but as it turns out this was a very painful endeavor, so i just scraped myself over and over with a safety pin. Cleo was brave. She lived in her own apartment off Hollywood Boulevard and took the subway to school every day. She was the most graceful 16 year old on the planet. She grabbed my hand at a party and pulled me into the bathroom. "You know they're all just jealous of you, right? That's why they're such bitches" she told me, in reference to the other girls in my grade.

And now I could feel it. She was never coming back. Still, I heard her voice in the wind and in every song. I prayed for the miracle of her return like we were war torn lovers. I saw her on every street corner, the way pious Christians swear they see Jesus in their mashed potatoes.

Or maybe I was just really high.

***** AND ME

This was the perfect out. The perfect escape. I hated Roman but I was a barnacle then, and there was no way to defy nature. Barnacles bond to their host until death. It was too horrific to imagine being alone, to imagine dying alone. I was born feeling very old. At 23 I felt 100, and who finds a new mate at 100? Best to just accept the cards I'd been dealt, and ride out my remaining 75 years with a guy who says "I want to fuck your mom" while he's inside me. 75 years is a breeze considering the amount of lifetimes I'd certainly lived. Once Roman told me he would dump me if I didn't buy him a pack of yellow American Spirits. I bought them. He told me he would break up with me if I didn't text my friends and tell them I hated them and never wanted to see him again. I texted. I called him hysterically crying once begging for him to take me back, and he looped my voicemail, turning it into a Timbaland-style hiphop beat.

"*I'm boggin' beggin' baby*

I'm begging baby wait"
Once Roman pinned me to the wall with
his forearm and spit in my face again
and again and again and again, and he
whipped me with a phone charger and
popped a blood vessel in my leg. He
threw my phone at the wall above my
head. There was a painting of a Chow
Chow on the wall and the phone hit the
painting and glass shattered on my skull
and blood gushed down my forehead
and I was really leaning into feeling faint
so he would feel extra guilty, even
though it didn't hurt at all. Not physically.
My failure to choose a worthwhile
romantic partner had created a soul
schism. The part of me begging to leave
despised the me that stayed and stayed.
I didn't trust myself to do anything
anymore. I felt like a twig holding a fat
bird, waiting to buckle. Snap.
But the right side of me, the side that
begged to be free, highjacked the
switchboard and accepted the call to
adventure when my friend Maya asked if
I wanted to take an interview to replace
her as *****'s assistant.

Is it breaking the NDA if I don't use his last name? What happens if you get sued and you have no money? The most expensive thing I own is the 2015 Macbook I'm typing this on, and ***** is an action star. What use would he have for all my half written creative nonfiction screenplays?

I never had a thing for pretty guys, mostly because they never had a thing for me. I knew who he was, everyone did, but I would never have considered myself a fan. That's like saying you're a fan of Mickey Mouse…it's implied. He was the punchline in every bad joke in every bad movie, and I was a punchline only to myself. The only thing we had in common was probably our weigh class. Of course he was 6'2' and all muscle, and I was 5'8" and all chili cheese tot.

After Roman fell asleep one night, I locked myself in the bathroom and watched interview after interview of *****. I watched him on Hot Ones and Jimmy Fallon and on Ellen. The fantasies started to swim without effort;

sperm towards the egg. ***** and I in a four wheeler in the United Arab Emirates.

"You have the Scorsese call today at 1:15, and Ice Spice is still waiting on your RSVP."

"Yes! Yes to EVERYTHING!" he'd tell me in his manic and agog way. I'd roll my eyes, the sardonic assistant. I was good at this.

 "I love you, Bellz. Do I tell you that enough?"

"Too much, I'm afraid." He'd ruffle my hair, then hop out of the four wheeler. "EH HEM!" I'd call after him, and toss him his sunglasses. He'd wink back, then go ride a motorcycle off a mountain.

After a week I received further instructions from Mae, *****'s sister, who was his executive assistant and my soon to be boss. I signed the NDA. The fantasies started to germinate and sprout.

We'd be off the Pacific coast in his sailboat, and the sun would be setting, and the lights of the coastline would be turning on one by one. We'd know that on the shore, families were gathering for fish and wine, teenage lovers were making out in a guest house, old couples were slow dancing to Nora Jones. We'd watch like angels, omnipresent and full of hope.

Two whales would rise from below, a mother and her calf. They'd splash us with their blowholes like erupting volcanoes. It is here that I am understood. ***** and I would cry and laugh because we are so full of love and life and because we have found each other and nothing makes any sense but it all adds up perfectly and tonight we will eat crab and fuck like monkeys and life will be that first weekend in June feeling forever.

I was in my apartment feverishly masturbating to the sailboat fantasy when I received an email with instructions for the interview.
An address to *****'s house in Bel Air.
Tomorrow, 7:30 AM.

7 alarms were set, the first one at 4:45 AM. There had to be time to meditate, do my Youtube ab workout, read, and do my hair and makeup, none of which I did when I woke up at 1 PM on normal days.

I drove up to a lookout point as the sun set on the final moments of my old little life. What a crazy beautiful ride it had been. A tear chilled my cheek. Fantasy ***** licked it off.

Going to sleep that night was a sort of going into labor. Lights were dimmed, candles lit, Gregorian chants played. It was my job to keep the atmosphere as soothing as possible. I did breath work and took a sleeping pill and after hours of tossing and turning, I drifted off to a new ***** fantasy.

We were live lobsters about to be dropped into a hot boiling pot, and we had lived so fully and so gorgeously that we weren't afraid, in fact we felt lucky that our flesh would be devoured as an expensive delicacy, side by side drenched in silky slippery warm. He clicks his antenna at me for the last time. We drop. Our screams harmonize, a holy hum, the final proof that we will meet again on the other side.

I awoke to shaking and wailing and a lump on my bed, sobbing in darkness. Roman.

"Is this real?" I asked him.
"I'm so sorry. I'm so sorry." Roman sniffled.
"What time is it?"
"2:30. I'm so sorry — "
"What happened?"
"You weren't answering your phone. I was so mad at you."
"What happened?"
"I was with Rob, he showed me this website called BackPages. You can —"
"What happened?"
"I...fucked someone. A hooker."

Hysteria ensued. I was less upset about the prostitute and more upset abut the fact that I was awake. I begged Roman to leave. Through weeps he whispered histrionically, "Can I please just…hold you for a minute?"

I slept dreamlessly, and when I gasped awake birds were mid song. Light snuck through the blinds. I scrambled for my phone.

It was on the floor untethered and dead next to the charger, Roman's phone plugged in in its place.

It was 7 AM. I had to be on the West Side in 30 minutes. I threw on the smart outfit from Target I had laid out. Roman slept with his mouth open. I glanced toward a pair of scissors, then back at his wide open mouth.
He wasn't worth it.

I started driving with my dead phone toward Bel Air. After 20 minutes it powered on. I texted *****'s sister from the 101 freeway.
"Good Morning, Mae! Stuck behind an accident. Running a few minutes behind. Terribly sorry."
"Drive safe :)" She replied.

But I was not driving safe. I could barely see. I could barely remember my own name. Images flashed. Pain. A whale with a harpoon through her eye. Screeching. Drowning. The ETA mounted and mounted.

"RRRRRRRRAAAAAAAAAAAAAAAAAA HHHHHHHHHPPPPPEEEUUUUGGk" Rocks of rage walloped my organs. The noises escaping me were satanic and cruel.

ETA: 7:42.

"Hi Mae! The freeway exit is shut down because of this accident. It's taking me on an alternate route now. Just my luck! :p"

ETA: 7:53.

"You seem lovely, but promptness and effective time management are such a

fundamental part of this position." Mae texted.
I picked up the phone immediately and called her.

"Hi, Bella."
"Mae, hi!"

At some point during the screaming, I had completely lost my voice.

"Hello? Bella? Are you there?"
"Can you hear me? I'm here. I'm here!" I squeaked to no avail.
She hung up. She texted.
"Sorry, Bella! We have a meeting with another candidate at 8. Wishing you all the best!"
"Sorry, I think my service is spotty. See you in a few!" I responded. There was too much at stake for me now. It was ***** or perish.

I peeled into the gate at 8:02. I entered the code that Mae had emailed. I entered it again. And again. And again. I watched from outside my body as I

punched and kicked the iron rodded
gate, the demons inside me howling on.
A security guard jogged at me.

"Mam, I've been instructed to let you
know that if you don't leave I have to call
the police to escort you off the property."

That night, with my hand down my
pants, ***** and I visited our friends
George and Amal Clooney at their home
in Lake Como. We had decided to nap
before dinner and woke to the sound of
their children laughing. The chef had
prepared a lobster feast. I fed him under
the Italian stars with lemon burning my
hangnails.

Feet stomped outside. Then the door
flung open.
"Why aren't you answering your phone,
you fat bitch?!" Roman asked.

OF LICE AND GIRLS

The sisterhood of the traveling parasite
red archways of popped guts in
notebook margins
How can you not look like sex
when bugs are fucking on your head

FIONA

Sixteen with EEE boobs, them nipples
blush pink yarmulkes
she said "I weigh myself then cut myself
then weigh myself"
rote as banana bread instructions.
A good girl seduced, a trust fund
squandered on Breakfast Jacks for 6

CLUNG

The 6 of us moved as a pack to the chagrin of our mothers, who were in a never ending game of Russian Roulette regarding whose house we would spend the night at. Since there were too many of us to fit in Sally's sedan, we would alternate which two would take turns riding in the black sweaty abyss of the trunk, faces mashed together, clung like koalas, swallowing each other's hysterical breath. We had one massive stolen Urban Outfitters wardrobe, shared one journal, washed each other in the shower, cut each others hair and pierced each other's noses. We fought for each other, with each other, held each other, housed each other, and often hated each other. The world was so tiny it felt like we held it in our pockets, but so big that everything was damp hair and benevolence and light. We were never not excited. Even when we were crying, even when Fiona had a tantrum because her dad took her step sister's side about the mysterious poisoning of the family toad Miley, even when Sasha took too much ecstasy and couldn't remember if she fucked Sock Jacobson's brother, even when my mom slept through most days and drank through most nights, we were excited. The world seemed to whisper "everything is about to change" and if ever that started to feel scary, we would carve our name into something. Trees, tables, benches, even each other. To be a teenage girl in 2008 meant taking up as little space as possible. We wrote our names on the world so it wouldn't forget us.

6 DAYS IN COUNTY

"I've been very very naughty", my
mother told me in her boyfriend's kitchen
on a summer afternoon, checking over
her shoulder for wandering ears.
"Want me to show you?"

She showed me, and by the next year I
was arrested for felony shoplifting. Turns
out my mother had become something
of a professional kleptomaniac. And it
turns out, as with most things, I just
wasn't as good as her.

At this point my best friend was Sally
Shapiro, a preschool teacher from
Orlando, Florida. Sally's eyes were
black and her voice was shrill and her
fingernails were wrapped in bandaids
from biting them off. On the night I was
apprehended, she screeched into the
parking garage of the Van Nuys Target
screaming to the cops —
"She's my girlfriend! Just let me kiss her
goodbye!"

She kissed me through the cop car window and as she did she rounded her lips into a funnel and launched a Xanax bar into my mouth with her tongue. I chewed it into a chalk and swallowed, nerve endings rounding, the moon coming a little closer, dolphins somewhere saying a prayer for me, crickets diddling harps and flutes, a home in my chest made of steel and honey and embers and chocolate.
We were drug addicts. We were 22. It was the year when all my friends were moving back home from college with the exception of Sally and I. I didn't go to college because it was too much paperwork and my mother didn't make me. Sally didn't go to college because she was stupid.
I had spent 4 years as a nanny and a personal assistant, I sold spa packages in department store parking lots. I became a "pizza artist" and I was the receptionist at a happy ending massage parlor. I was a production assistant on a web series about Call of Duty. I worked at Madewell at the 3rd street promenade and got fired for giving Maude Apatow

free leggings. I supported my deadbeat
boyfriend. I lost all of my friends. I got
sad. I got fat. I took pills. I felt the world
and I had a score to settle. I felt the
world owed me…stuff. So I stole it.
All of it: mango milk candles, coconut
waters, jeggings, stuffed animals,
Wolfgang Puck sandwiches, blenders,
down comforters, sushi, headphones,
grapes, lamps, stamps, perfumes, beta
fish, fake blood, jewelry, mugs, saucers,
shrimp cocktails, diet soda and Buddha
shaped piggy banks.

There was a basement under the
courthouse where I waited to be
transferred to County. In the basement
was a girl gang from Palmdale that had
robbed Theresa's ex boyfriend at gun
point. Theresa was the gang's leader.
She had Russian red hair and a smile
like the Cheshire Cat and eyeliner like a
sexy cartoon spider. I started to
fantasize that maybe we would fall in
love or that she'd make me her bitch.

They moved us to Lynwood County Jail at dawn. I spread my asshole open for a buxom woman in a khaki uniform. I coughed. I thought, "you've come a long way from Malibu Methodist Preschool" Then I ate a bean and cheese burrito, drank a chocolate milk, and slept for 22 hours.

I was still high when I woke up, thank God. Something slept on the bunk below me, but it's face was buried in a pillow. There was a bible next to my bed so I started to read it. Eventually I heard a wild cackling. The thing below me was Jinx, my first cellmate. Jinx etched anime characters into the bed with the plastic fork that came attached to her fruit cup. Jinx and I were the same age. I tried to connect with Jinx on that.

We didn't leave the cell at all for 3 days, except for once to get an intake physical.
"Are you addicted to street drugs of any kind?" The doctor asked.
"I'm addicted to Xanax."

"Is that prescribed to you by a doctor or
you get it on the street?"
I realized in this moment I had the heart
of a rat. If it meant freedom, I would
have narced on my dealer right then and
there. I was fucking him. I didn't care.
"Street."
The doctor shook her head.
"You know that stuff will kill you, yeah?"
"I guess so."
"I'll give you 5 mg of Klonopin daily."

I was high as hell all weekend, reading
the bible on my bunk like a kid at sleep
away camp after lights out. Finally on
Sunday, we were allowed out for church.
I felt God beating his tiny drum behind
my corneas and in the back of my
throat. I listened to him play for a while. I
was happy to see an old friend.

On Monday I was finally permitted
phone access. My brother was at an
Oscar party.
"It was crazy, they announced that La La
Land won, but really it was Moonlight.
It's a whole thing. It was crazy. I felt so

bad for Damien Chazelle. Can you imagine?"
"Who the fuck is that!?" his influencer girlfriend yelled in the background.

On movie night we watched Monster-In-Law starring Jane Fonda and Jennifer Lopez. Everyone hated Jane Fonda's character. When something bad would happen to her they'd whoop and cheer. "THAT'S WHAT YOU GET YOU STUPID BITCH!!!"

Jinx was transferred so I had the cell to myself one evening.
At this point in my life there was a boy who would not love me back. I covered myself in the state issued blanket like a cadaver, closed my eyes, and imagined the boy stood at the foot of my cell, blood caked and sweating from the hundreds of cops he murdered breaking in to rescue me. I came 3 times.

Erin was my next cellmate. Erin who wouldn't stop crying. I thought of the slippery red salamanders I'd hunt with

my mother in Eaton Canyon. Erin swore
she didn't do anything wrong.
I promised her things would get better.
That seemed like the only option.

And they did.

By now, the world has settled the score.
By now, the world has paid me back
with interest. It has given me lobster in
various wharfs and a lover who spoon
feeds me pudding. I have friends who I
look up to and a home office and dogs
who lick me dry after the shower. I have
been in movies, made movies, been to
Switzerland, and had my feet sucked by
fish.

My mother used to say I have Never
Enough Syndrome. Maybe that's why I
still crave the bean and cheese burrito I
had on my first night in jail. Why I crave
the girl I was. Why I crave being
shameless and slimy and ratlike. No one
expects much of you when you're trying
to out disgust yourself, trying to outrun
the ache with a cart full of Target sheet

sets and a drug dealer who you occasionally blow.

Some days missing Rat Queen makes it impossible to do anything. Rat Queen did not know what was cool. Rat Queen did not care about careers or how to get more followers or politics or death. Rat Queen loved Beyoncé and athleisure wear and "Sunday Funday" and crunchy fall leaves. She purloined and plundered and pouted and promised her heart and always meant it.

I look at my face and I am haunted by the lack of pudge in my cheeks, I lift up my shirt and I am haunted by the white stretch marks that for Rat Queen glistened pinks and purples like a winter sunset.
Rat Queen, my sunset. Without you the home in my chest is moth balls and plastic and apologies and fire. Without you I have become a jester, desperately appealing to a court that doesn't care about my heart of hope, my home stolen deities, the gunk and slop that makes me shimmer.

NOTES ON THE TWINS

It's hard to choose my favorite twin. One is the tomboy twin, one is the girly twin. Those are the rules. The twins are like two albino koi fish dancing circles around each other, tales fanning and flirting in the moonlight. The twins always call each other ugly even though they are identical twins. The twins have been shaving their vaginas since the 5th grade. "They start even younger in South Africa." The twins are South African but they talk like cholas. The twins and I hitchhiked home from the Galleria with a 40 year old Armenian man named Gor who asks, "where the orgy at?" The twins mother beats them with a hairbrush.

MEXICO

She says, "I don't know who I am
outside of my desperation for the world's
approval". Accidental eye contact is
made with the half dug up lobster on her
plate. She adds "I can feel myself doing
it without my own consent, morphing
into what I think the person in front of
me wants to see."
He swigs something, then says, "it's so
fucking hot when you talk to me like
this."

DREAM FLUFF

In my sleep I meet the lovers of my past in dimly lit restaurants, in old timey train cars, in the homes of my childhood. My lovers are angular and not without agenda. They share a seaside cottage with koi fish ceilings and round the clock pot roasts and they wait there to feed me, to teach me to dance. Often they smell like places and times, my grandparent's stable (1997), wet night park bark (2008). Often they demand answers. I swear the answers are coming. I kiss each of them goodnight.

I only like things that are no longer there, dream fluff, like yesterday, like places and people that are dead dead dead. I douse my skin in honey and sing their special song and they come and they feed, like the lovers in the seaside cottage, like Malibu 2002 and deli cuts and pesto and my mother in a cable knit, I could really fall in love with something like that, but not with my destiny that stands before me and makes me a promise, not with a creaky

crusty future and it's greasy slick of
always, but with lovers in my dreams
who suck me of tomorrow, and leave me
a fuzzy pink pork bun in love with the
world.

BOOMER HUMOR

This feels a little like a first date. I'm clearing my throat too much. There are pebbles in it.

"Soooo, what do you do?" I kid. She doesn't think this is funny. That's fine. It was a risky joke and my mother wasn't funny when she was alive, so I doubt much has changed in that department.

My mother's humor was so boomer that it threatened my very existence. Her sense of humor was just a series of dance moves (i.e."The White Man's Underbite") and quotes from unmemorable movies starring Ben Affleck. The "talking to the dead parent" scene in movies is always so cathartic and sexy. In our final mutually corporeal convo, my mom told me she was praying for me and I told her she was a sociopath and blocked her number. Needless to say, catching up now is a bit uncomfortable.

My phone rings and my heart stops as if it's her calling. It was never fun to feel my phone buzz and look down to see my mother's name. She was always either mad at me, asking me to lie for her, or sitting with one of her stupid ass friends who simply NEEDED to hear my Fat Bastard impression. By the time she died I had her stored in my phone as HATER with the sunglasses emoji and a peace sign. Decline!!! My mom was the best at screening calls. She always let them ring all the way through and carried on with her glass of cheap wine.

"Mom, aren't you gonna get that?"
"Nope."
"Why?"
"Because I don't want to."

When I was 23 she called me and said "I was just watching Saturday Night Live and I came up with a plan. You're going to be the next Melissa McCarthy." This was a great day for my mom because she got to call me funny and fat in the same breath, her two favorite pastimes.

What can I say to her now? Maybe I should just make her laugh. Although she wasn't funny, she really was a beautiful audience. My kindergarten best friend Moon and I used to do RENT soundtrack sing offs and make our families vote for who was better. It was completely sadistic on my part since Moon was a natural performer with a voice like a choir boy's. But my mom always voted for me even though everyone else voted for Moon, which made the veins in Mom's forehead throb. Once she even booed Moon and called her voice "soulless". Moon wept and wept and it was awesome.

I wish I could tell you this was the only time she had beef with a child on my behalf. Once she pushed this girl China Lennox into a Fruitoopia machine for calling me a "pork sandwich". That night the cops showed up to my house and threatened to arrest my mom for child abuse. She answered the door with my baby brother on her hip and charmed her way out of it. Obviously.

I was in the 3rd grade and my mom was 8 months pregnant when she waddled up to notorious school bully Alonzo Karvukian, who had yet again spent recess following me around singing a song comprised of my name, fart sounds, and the sounds of women cumming.

"Do you know who I am?"

Alonzo was shaking. "You're Bella's mom."

"Yeah, and you're on my shit list."

It was truly hilarious but I knew better than to laugh. For my mother this was serious business, plus she could NOT laugh at herself. Once I made fun of her fake boobs. I told her that me and my brothers are all stupid because silicone trickled into our milk supply. She didn't speak to me for 6 months.

I, on the other hand, insist on being the butt of every joke. I spent 6th grade playing a game called "invisibilia" in which I spent hours being completely ignored while all the other kids talked shit about me. I would scream obscenities in their faces, desperate to get them to smile. I have been tied up, taped, ditched, slapped, table-topped and tea bagged, all for the glint in their eyes that said "Wow, she's crazy! Look what she's letting me do to her!" (Of course, they never realized the show was for me, not them.)

But now I'm in the car and I'm talking to my dead mom and I can't think of anything funny to say, not even at my own expense. This is the same reason I will not commit to Twitter. When I'm trying to be funny it just shuts off, like trying to be good at kissing or saying your name too many times in the mirror. If only I could text her. If TEXTING my mother beyond the grave were an option, I'd pen her a sermon so hilarious God and The Devil would be left breathless and pink cheeked.

I hate this. I've become one of those people who hates confrontation which makes me hate myself. I've logged my genius hours on Instagram watching reels of bathing primates and crispy parmesan potatoes. The screens have made me too limp clitted and riddled with placation to have an actual honest conversation with anyone. It doesn't matter if they stand before me hot and fleshy or if they're a ghost playing passenger princess in the front seat of my Corolla.

Although this wasn't true when she was alive, I can't shake the feeling that if I could just hear her voice one more time, if I could just hear my mom make an egregiously unfunny joke, I would be okay. Because right now I am not okay. My OCD has gotten so bad that I rub hand sanitizer on my feet every time I enter the house. Some nights I'm afraid to fall asleep out of fear I'll never wake up. The rituals are mangling me, taking up more and more time. I must wipe 20 times at least. Nothing can be done less than 18 times because that is legal adult age and if I do it less than 18 times I am a pedophile. My world feels completely uninhabitable.

I keep remembering this OCD flare up I had when I was 14 where I had nonstop beastiality themed intrusive thoughts. I would be doing my homework and suddenly flashes of me sucking our 16 year old bichon frisee's red rocket would strangle me whole. Me eating out a baby girl kitten. Me getting fucked by a horse. An anxiety so excruciating that I could barely eat, and when I did eat I puked it up. I missed 2 weeks of school and I locked myself in my room to protect society (and our dog) from myself. A true martyr. The Joan of Ark of Sherman Oaks.

During this era, the only compulsion that temporarily staved off the beastiality thoughts was having every label of every product facing away from me. Every couple of hours a knock would come at my bedroom door accompanied by an impish "Beeeeelllllaaaa".

I'd open up to find my mom standing there with my little brother peaking out behind her legs. She'd be holding a shampoo bottle or a box of cereal like a cross during an exorcism, label pointed right at me. She and my little brother would laugh hysterically. I'd scream and cry and slam the door in her face.

But after a few days, I looked forward to the knock. Through her eyes I could make sense of myself.

Maybe she was funny. Maybe I'm more like her than I realize, and maybe that's the reason the world without her scares me so much. She tethered me, for better or worse, to the person she believed me to be. Funny and bright and fat and evil. Without her it's up to me to decide, and maybe I've decided I'm not funny at all.

I let the silence curl around us.

I open my mouth to speak —

FOR PARISA

For Parisa
forever, and for her hair
for Parisa in Paris,
if she ever made it there.
For Parisa's Persian pussy in Paris
And for the thick palomino
pelt that sprung from her
scalp the baby hairs
that sucked on her
neck O! tender onyx leeches
She was more than a Chipotle employee
Her acrylics caked with sour cream
She said
"I'm moving to Paris, bitch!
Don't worry, you'll see!"
Praying Parisa's neck hairs are
sucking and fucking
beneath the glow of the Eiffel
A sloppy kiss of sweat and jojoba oil
I hope they know their mother's
dream came true
A dream we spit
and shook on
in the Tarzana Chipotle
parking lot

NATALIA

There are many sad things, but by far the saddest is that my children will never know the way your limbs flail when you dance, the way you suck your gummy worms to sludge, your fat knuckles, the way you tease, your perfect cupids bow, or your stupid ass hats, and it's not because you died, and it's not because we fell out of love. My children will never meet their aunt because I fucked her ugly ass boyfriend in the back of a Ford Fiesta, which means I failed them long before they were born, because to know Natalia is to know everything.

ATLANTIS

The rest of my life I will be waiting to die
so I can be born again. Life is a long line
for the roller coaster, being 17 is the
actual ride. Everything that follows is in
sentimentality and every second that i
am not 17 i am dead and disgusting, i
am road kill, liver freckled and feckless.
Being 17 is the food fresh from the
kitchen, parsley dusted and candle lit.
Being 30 is that same meal postmated
and microwaved 3 days later. It is
edible, sure, but one consistency (mush)
and most notably, cold in random spots.

I found myself masturbating to images
of Olivia Rodrigo fucking my 40 year old
boyfriend last week. Her taught tan
body, her ass cheeks like a halved
pomelo, ride the boyfriend's sleepy old
cock, his ass cheeks sloshing like two
ziplock bags of milk. It is his honor to
house her hole, to protect and to teach.
But she teaches him too. He is a feeble
explorer, before him the underwater lost
city of Atlantis. She rides and barnacles
bolt her mouth closed, baby seahorses

rocket from her ears. She bends for him, slow, and sucks the fish eggs from his tip. 1, 2, 3, 4…slow like honey. He cums for 45 minutes. He has never c*m, not truly, until this moment. Because sex with me is not Atlantis. It is a strip mall in North Hollywood. It is the "ACCIDENTES? CALL (800)444-4444" ad on the back of the Metro. My mouth is exhausted from exhaust exposure so my sucker hangs limp and juiceless, reeking of 7/11 sausage biscuit.

But for my boyfriend this is a good life. He is a simple man who favors convenience, pleasures close to home. He loves the city that birthed me, and he loves it in me, and he loves sausage biscuits, and he is afraid of most things, of heights too high and depths too deep, so for him Atlantis would be panic inducing.
But I can't erase what I know about being young. When the seamen would whisper about their semen and promise to be the first ones to make me cum, and they'd beg and beg for my tiny belly full of eels. They loved that it was

wicked to want me, and I understand as I picture Olivia sucking my imaginary cock. Or Billie Eillish. Or Millie Bobby Brown. I love feeling like a fat king, King Triton. I love fisting them with anything I can find, sea cucumbers, flounder, tentacles of all shapes and sizes. I can't pretend I don't know how good it feels to be carded at the liquor store, to be dubbed "jailbait", to make the days and months and years of old pathetic men with the curl of my kisser. All I can do now is remember. And imagine, and request my boyfriend call me a "good little girl" when he fucks the ever expanding B rated Chinese Restaurant in the corner of my strip mall, and pray for a death as hasty and flower crowned as girlhood itself.

TEENAGE SEMEN

The summer after our freshman year I met Yoni and by August I had fallen desperately in love for the first time, spending my days eating chicken salad sandwiches and making love in a slew of bank parking lots. The girls would call, I would decline. I was addicted to the way he looked at me and to the horrible feelings taking root inside my chest, wounds I had not yet been forced to examine. I was addicted to feeling like I would absolutely die without him. I was addicted to the excruciating inevitability that some day we would break up, and to the stories I'd heard about high school sweethearts growing old together. "When you know, you know!" All the women would say, and I aspired to be a woman who knew something. I was addicted to dedicating songs to him and comparing our love story to those of the greats. I was addicted to how jealous the girls seemed to be. They all wanted boyfriends, even though Cleo would never have admitted she did.

Everyday I felt like one of those people who wins a radio contest, and through tears cries "I've never won anything before!" I would kiss Yoni hard, eyes fixed on my naked body reflected in his mirrored closet door. I would watch the teepee pitch in his boxer briefs because of things I knew how to do. Lick, pet, whisper, repeat. Finally, I knew how to do something. I was addicted to feeling powerful. I'd never been powerful before. I was a 15 year old girl with chub rub and blistered feet tangled in a California summer, spinning teenage semen into spools of gold. Name one thing more powerful. I'll wait.

THE CRISIS OF
MY LARGENESS

It is my God given right to be a baby, to be pet and primped, fondled and fought for. Helpless and insufferable and coddled by candlelight when the sugar dusted sweet treats and foig gras won't take, when the tub full of tuberose makes me too sad, I must remind you that I was born to be an infant, so tiny even the insects want to swaddle and hush me, even the germs want to read me Goodnight Moon.

So you can understand the crisis of my largeness. You can understand the pain of having the meat of me work against everything I've ever wanted. The insects who wish to swaddle buckle beneath the weight of me and they are dead and it is my fault. The sweet treat and foig ras will send me over my Weight Watcher's points budget. There is no one to bathe or defend me due to man's twisted formula that big equals brave. Hello you idiots, I am a BABY! What is it that you don't understand? I wish not for bravery or honor, I wish for a warm baba and a succulent titty and a man, a man who scoops me up and wipes me off and tells me I have his eyes, the eyes of the Maccabees, of blood on the walls and locusts and triumph and togetherness, the eyes of a family. But I am a baby battling a perfect storm of forest fires and immolation in a world that outgrows me with each sprouting grey.

Other dreams are cast aside as my sole focus lie in shrinking. I must return to baby size for you. Don't worry, I won't make you say it. I am devoted to my infancy. I live on protein shakes and string cheese and the annual shrinking begins. I usually see it in my face first, then my arms, and if I'm pious enough my tummy starts to hollow and melt. "172.4" sings the scale. "She's so cute" sing the men on the street. I giggle at the sun. "You are perfect" echoes the world. I am happy, so happy, too happy, so I do what happy babies do. I rejoice.

I clutch a smashed banana in my fist. I
eat tenders and am tender. Then a short
stack, as a reward. Then a Big Mac, as
a treat. Burrito. Lox bagel. I have to live,
don't I? I deserve to freakin' live.

Then I cry and cry. No one comes to
swaddle and coddle. "203.4" the scale
hisses. "You have failed" hiss the girls
on TikTok. I am back to where I started,
a guilt too inconceivable.

This year it will be different, though. Or
next year. Or the year after that. But
some day I will be strong enough to
change for good, to be so small you'll
have no choice but to make me your
baby.
The worst thing in the world to miss.

THE IMMORTAL RUMOR OF THE GREAT BUTTFUCKING

The Great Buttfucking was the beginning of the end for Rachel and I.

I had always been a devout girl friend, praying to wavy tendrils and secret keeping. Romantic love felt like checkers. Platonic love felt like chess. It was an art, a skill, something sacrosanct. And I was good at it.

Rachel was the first person I loved that wasn't family. The first person I ever decided to love, loved by choice. Though it never really felt like a choice.

On the day we met she was wearing a neon yellow raincoat and a bedazzled tee that said SPOILED GIRL. She spun around outside our second grade classroom in the rain. We bonded over our our favorite pastime, adult situation role play with a magical realism twist: cheating husband caught making love to a fairy, abused housewife falls in love with her pop star centaur neighbor, mom and daughter dance battle for the love of most powerful warlock. We were dolphins together (wink, you can stop reading now). And witches. And unicorn husband and wife, humping in her grandmother's Palm Springs guest room under the flickering light of the infomercial channel.

Sometimes it was hard to tell if I was in love with her or just wanted to be her. In middle school her hip bone was stained with the Playboy bunny, the puffy tissue surrounding it burnt tanning salon orange. She'd always yell comic book onomatopoeias like "WHAPISH! PHEEWP! SMUCH!" and kick me in the legs or slap me as hard as possible on the back. I would scream in agony and she would pee her leggings laughing, a game enjoyed by both players.

Sometimes she broke my heart, like when she told me I had boobs like a chimpanzee. Sometimes I broke hers, like when I got fingered by her boyfriend Joseph Peretti during The Exorcism of Emily Rose. But we always came back stronger, better.

That was until The Great Buttfucking.

The Great Buttfucking was a rumor being passed around my middle school that I let this fat boy with a blue mohawk, Ace, fuck me in the ass. The Great Buttfucking was fake news. The truth was this: on the floor of his pool house, Ace sandwiched his flaccid little penis between my butt cheeks and boinged up and down, sucking saliva back through the rubber bands in his braces. We thought this meant butt sex. Why wasn't it painful? I googled butt sex a few weeks later to discover the truth. *There had been NO Great Buttfucking!* But by then, it was too late. Ace had told the entire school about the encounter. Obviously.

"I heard your eyes rolled back into your skull" Said Harrison Woods.

"I heard you got a little fleck of poo on
his penis!" Said Victoria Dominguez.

*"My butt! My butt my butt my butt!
Sure, you can fuck this butt.
Check it out!"*
The boys on the 8th grade lawn sang to
the tune of My Humps by the Black
Eyed Peas.

Rachel and I never lied to each other.
"It's just weird that you said you did…
and now you're saying you didn't?"
"Rachel, I didn't know."
"How is that possible? Are you fucking
braindead?"
Her betrayal slowly gave way to hate.
She tagged ASS WH<3RE on the locker
that we once shared. I knew it was her
from the heart shaped O. She sent me
the song "Somebody that I Used to
Know" by Elliot Smith on Myspace.

I groomed a girl from 3rd period choir, a
bean pole French girl named Maxine
Charles, into being my new best friend. I
thought her all the Rachel tricks. It
wasn't the same.

Rachel and I went on to the same high school. She joined drama academy. We said "hi" in the hallways and it was always a little sad. She became best friends with Sarah Mitzkovich. Her uncle was Danny Elfman and she was rumored to have a roast beef pussy. Ace, the great buttfucker, went to our school, too. He maintained that we took each other's virginities.

After high school Rachel moved to New York. I checked in on her online from time to time. She went to NYU. Eventually she started dating a blond guy named Jack Mulligan. Then they got engaged.

One day in 2022, all of the photos of Jack Mulligan were deleted off Rachel's Instagram. Shortly after, I received this DM:

"I've been going through my past and working on my relationship with my own sexual trauma. I want to say I'm so sorry I weaponized your assault against you. I remember feeling deeply triggered because I thought you were lying to me, but now I understand the importance of always believing the victim. "

Had I been…assaulted?

"Well, only you can answer that. Was it consensual?" My therapist, Lisa, asked.
"It wasn't anything. We didn't have sex."
"Heard. And believed. That said, was it consensual?"
"Yes."
"You explicitly gave him permission?"
"I mean, I was 13. Probably not."
"If you don't explicitly give permission, some might consider that to be assault."
"Well I don't, because it wasn't anything! We didn't have sex!"
"Okay, but let's say you did—"
"WE DIDN'T!"

"Right."

PALLBEARERS

My first love and my last love, buzzard
beaked bookends, the only two whose
aims were true. For the first I was a bare
child, and for the last I will bear child,
then together they will bear the pall
when my baring days are through.

MORTIMER'S BACKPACK

Mortimer was the worst kind of rotten kid, a rotten kid with absolutely lovely parents, so you knew the rottenness was nature, not nurture, which made empathizing with him impossible. He was not puny and he was not large (the two leading elementary school death sentences), he had plenty of friends named Hudson and Phoenix, he had Fortnite posters fanned across his room which was bigger than my entire apartment, and he had me, delivering him honey toast and taquitos while he watched Youtube videos of teenagers shooting each other with air soft guns.

Mortimer's parents met in college and both worked in the legal department at Netflix. In Los Angeles, this is as wholesome as a family gets. They were constantly offloading their swag to me and in the 6 months I worked for them I got a Stranger Things oven mitt, an Umbrella Academy mug, and a hoodie from the movie The Kissing Booth that I wore almost every day.

When we played games Mortimer would scream "BOOOOOM" in my face when I lost, and when I won he would throw himself on the ground, sobbing, and with all his might he'd rip grass out of the yard and throw it all over his head screaming "YOU CHEATED" his golden skin gone tomato red. I'm not sure why he'd dress himself with the grass but I can only guess it was all part of some self-flagellation ritual he subconsciously performed when he felt embarrassed. It was not hard to imagine that in previous lives Mortimer participated in or frankly invented humiliating ways of punishing people. Whenever I drove him to baseball practice, a 35 minute drive each way, he would make me play Michael Jackson's Thriller over and over and over again, and if I refused he would kick the back of my chair and sing a song called "POOP ASS MEAN ASS STUPID ASS BITCH" until I complied. "You know, Michael Jackson was a really bad person." I said on the drive

one day, just to watch the little veins in his little forehead bulge.
"NO!"
"Yes. He did lots of evil things to little kids. Kids like you."
"NO! HE DIDN'T! HE RAN AN AMUSEMENT PARK!"
"The amusement park was a trick. That's how he got the little boys there to do bad things to them."
"SHUT UP! LIAR! BITCH!"

In the same way you can't reason with a crazy person, you can't reason with a spoiled little boy. I didn't care enough about him to try to mold him into a nice man. I did worry that my future daughters or my friend's future daughters might be roofied by him in 20 years, but this was unlikely since he lived all the way in Arcadia. I accepted that I was getting paid to drive around a future terrible person with a fruit punch Hitler mustache.

Until I started to love him. He was sweet in flickers. "Tell me a story about when you were a kid" he asked one bedtime, and I told him about the rodeo with my grandparents, and how when we got back to their Galveston beach house I put on a rodeo of my own right there in the sand using a driftwood log as a cow. I watched his brain mulling and twisting. The next day Morty said "Whatever you do, do NOT look outside!" When he came back in he giggled "I have a surprise for ya!" And he blindfolded me and led me out the front door. He had set up a rodeo for us on his front lawn.

I started to teach him pleases and thank yous. "We don't want him to say it unless he really *means* it." Morty's mom told me. It was time to cut her out of the picture as far as the rearing of her son was concerned. He started to hold eye contact when he asked for something. He put his napkin in his lap. Something was swelling in my stomach…pride? Joy?

Mortimer and his sister, Liza, who was 5'10" and 13 and just as lovely as her parents, attended a private Catholic school in Calabasas. I picked them up from school most afternoons.

It was an unbearably hot September afternoon. I was picking up Liza, Morty, and Morty's dumb ass friend with a lisp, Milo. As we walked back to my car through the parking lot, Mortimer took his backpack off and dropped it in front of me without looking.
"Hold this." Was all he said before continuing his conversation with Milo about Roblocks.
"No."
"Just take it."
"No. No way."
"PLEASE!!!!!!!!!!!!!!"
"No. You can carry your own backpack today."
"I SAID PLEASE!"
"And I appreciate that. But I'm not carrying it. I'll carry it tomorrow if you ask me nicely." His beady eyes started darting around. "You can leave it there

to get run over or pick it up and walk to the car."
He collapsed, wailing in the middle of the parking lot. No traffic could pass through. Kids and parents stared. The crossing guard ask if we were okay.
"Get up, Morty."
"YOU. WILL. TAKE. THE. BACKPACK."
Liza's panicked eyes swelled with embarrassment. "Here Morty, I'll take the backpack—"
"There you go, Morty. Your sister will take it. Get up—"
"NO! IT HAS TO BE YOU!!!!!!"
Liza grabbed the backpack and began to trot off, humiliated. Morty gathered himself off the ground. He charged at Liza with a guttural war cry. He snatched his backpack off her shoulder. He laid back down in the middle of the road.
I grabbed Mortimer, furious. I knew myself enough to know I was about to do something crazy.
"MORTY!"
"YOU!!!!!! NO ONE ELSE. WE'RE. NOT. LEAVING. UNLESS. YOU. TAKE. THE. — —"

A perfect spiral. A direct hit. The fat wad
of gum I spit in his direction lay on the
concrete in front of him. Time freezes.
He cups his eye. A piercing yelp restarts
the clock. Concerned parents swarm in
concern. Mortimer's eye is swollen shut.
There is puss. Milo pisses his pants.
The paramedics arrive. We ride in the
ambulance. Morty thrashes around in
agony. Liza is sobbing. She looks at me
with fear and hatred. The parents are
called. The mother's voice is raised. She
is on her way. Mortimer kicks and
screams in the hospital bed. The nurses
hold him down. He says he cannot see.
They give him a shot. He settles. He
asks to play Minecraft on his tablet.

"I thought you couldn't see."
"OUT OF THE LEFT EYE I CAN!"
"How do you ask?"
"MAY I HAVE MY TABLET, PLEASE?'

MARES

I finally get why the women in my family
were never meant to stick together, but
to leap from their mothers without
panties or nets. I must have a daughter
whose sleepy eyes I will inhale. I must
drink her at her smelliest and her holiest
and when she laughs I must remember
why I give her my mother's name, and
while her father sleeps I must stay up
with her until dawn, my cousin CJ in her
lips, my aunt Sarah in her eyes, and
together we'll paint the women in my
family, which she'll do with her daughter,
and her daughter will do with her's, and
on and on until the study of this lineage
has raised an army of mothers and
daughters who are best friends and
mean it, mothers and daughters who
men on the street assume are lovers,
who call, who stay, who forgive, who
squeeze and suck and fuck life until
their blue in the face then ride into the
sunset naked together on palomino
speckled mares, mothers and daughters
that don't need you or anyone else to tell
them they're wonderful painters, and
then it'll really be over for you bitches.

HUBBY CAM

Before her, a girl had never farted in front of me. Sometimes I have flashbacks to the night we first kissed, then I blink and it's 9 years later and I'm putting in her tampon for her as she giggles. She loves to shock and disgust me. She texts me photos of her poop. I wonder if her disgustingness is her way of making sure I'm strong enough. Last night she came out of the bathroom with period blood on her face. "YOU KISS ME! ME WOMAN!" She yipped. I gagged. Her armpits smell like hot trash and grilled onions. I miss her when she goes to the bathroom.

FUCK STINK

I had just been fired from my hostessing job in Sherman Oaks because I asked Alec Baldwin for a selfie, and because I was in love with a fat assed graphic design student with buck teeth who went to UC Santa Barbara. I was out of town most weekends visiting him when they needed me at the restaurant most. Since I was gone on the weekends, my next job would need to be a weekday job. My mom was changing the locks on me at least once a month, and the twitch in her eye that used to come after midnight now commenced at 4PM. I would go up to her room to check on her, and she'd be watching tv the way a dog does where you're not sure if they're actually watching or if they're just staring at the dancing lights and colors. I would call her name from her doorway, and she would turn her head toward me sloooowly, like Linda Blair in the Exorcist. I was terrified. I was certain of only one thing: money was how I freed myself from her, and from the Chanel

No. 5 that seeped from the carpet, and from my little brother's loose turds clogging my toilet. I was horny out of my mind for anything that sounded remotely "normal" or "adult" but really I just wanted something — anything — stable.

Out of the blue, I received an email from my mom's old boyfriend, Jim. The subject line read "no subject".

Jim had been hired to write an animated pilot for Cartoon Network about international super spy raccoons and needed a fast typist to come type for him while he dictated. He offered me $12 dollars an hour and made me promise not to tell my mother. This made sense. Last I checked they were not on speaking terms.

A few years prior, I was going through my mom's emails, as I often did.

jim5dogs@aol.com:
Romy,
I know you're gonna tell me to go fuck myself. But I'm gonna say what I need

to say anyway, because frankly I think everyone else is too afraid of you to say what they're all, yes darling, ALL, thinking…
You're SICK!!!! You're a drug addict and an alcoholic and you're killing yourself slowly. The last time I saw you I noticed you had a bald spot.I can only assume it's because you're rotting from the inside. What happened to that sweet southern belle I met in '99? The girl in the polka dots who smelled like sunshine?
Again, I know you're gonna respond with some big fuck you. And that's fine. At least I have the satisfaction of knowing I tried.
romytexas63@aol.com: FUCCKadv YOUUUUUcksjbdcv

Jim was the only boyfriend of my mothers I had ever really enjoyed. He built superhero action figures, wore turquoise jewelry, and spoke like a sloth on a ventilator. He let me climb all over him and put half a stick of butter in my oatmeal. He took me to see Mulan in theaters and we laughed together and cried together. I loved him, I really did. I loved that he talked to me like an adult and that our house smelled like patchouli and wet dog when he came over. I couldn't wait to see him again. It had been 10 years, and I was exhausted from my expedited launch into womanhood. Perhaps Jim could offer some sort of respite from this…

At Jim's house there were throw pillows with the Green Lantern symbol on them and random tubs of flavored Psyllium Husk powder in each room. I showed up on my first day in my mom's kitten heels and Jim led me to the kitchen where he was making breakfast for his 5 dogs. Kibble, fried eggs, pinto beans, raw broccoli, a blue pill for Penny and Libby, a pink pill for Murdy, and about a gram of crumbled up brown marijuana each. "Keeps them mellow while I'm working. Come, check this out."
In his closet, billows of weed hung in bouquets upside down. Sad, dry, and slumped there in the darkness like cadavers, he was proud of each of them. Something about the way he

looked at them lit a fire in me that
needed him to be proud of me, too. I
had to do a good job.

After an hour and a half of watching Jim
putter about, we sat down to work. Jim
sat across from me on a black leather
sofa with Murdy at his feet, his hand
wrapped around his juicy Dalmation
skull. I put on a pair of my mom's old
readers I found in a junk drawer to seem
serious. I cracked my knuckles and
gestured at cracking my neck even
though I had never successfully done so
in my life. Libby, a Pekinese, hopped up
onto my lap.

"Okay, new document —"

"My dentist raped me, you know. I was 5
years old."

A horrific and eternal silence followed.

All I could say was —
"I'm so sorry."
"Did it to a bunch of kids. He gave them
laughing gas then just…went to town. All

the other kid's families testified against him in court, but *my* mother wouldn't let *me* testify. That was my mother. She hated me because she wanted a girl. Once she beat me so bad I couldn't see for 3 days. The skin around my eyes turned green and was so swollen and leaking with so much puss. She told the ER I was bit by a snake. The poetry."

Most days went on like this. He told me of the abysmal horrors not just of his own life, but of everyone's, of the dangers of people and society at large. Casual statements like —

"The water supply is full of feces and mercury. The governments main goal is to kill Jews and black people. I hope kill me sooner rather than later. I can't bare much more of the loneliness."
"Your mother is a whore. A terrible person, but an even worse actress. She sucks dick like a vacuum cleaner though, so she gets away with it."
"You gotta have what I call FUCK STINK. It's a scent people can pick up, not just women, men too. Let's them

know you been fucking, and you been fucking good. That's the only way a man will want to fuck you, let alone love you. You've got to have FUCK STINK. Now my FUCK STINK's all dried up. The only thing I fuck is microwaved cantaloupe."

Had he always been this way and hidden it from me, or was 10 years all it took to drive a man hideous? I was more depressed for myself than anything. What a luxury to be a baby, to have the world only show you the best version of itself.

Quitting wasn't an option. He was so desperate for human connection; I couldn't bare the thought of leaving him. But sometimes I really, really needed a break. I called in sick once so I could go to the beach with a few of my girl friends.
Jim texted:
"Next time you decide to LIE TO ME, remind your subconscious that I am NOT your father."

I went up to Santa Barbara one
weekend to visit my fat assed lover. We
went to a kegger on Isla Vista street,
and over Party Rock Anthem by
LMFAO, my lover screamed -
"QUIT! Are you dumb? This guy sounds
like a fucking psychopath. He probably
just wants to fuck you." At least now Jim
and I had loneliness in common.

I got home from SB on Sunday at 2AM.
My phone chimed. It was Jim.
"DON'T COME 2MORROW. MURDY
DYING."
I flopped down onto my bed, but my
head landed on something damp. There
was a salty, savory smell. I reached my
hand into my pillowcase. My little
brother had filled all of my pillows with
cold cut ham. I looked up and there was
ham on the wings of my ceiling fan.
There was ham on my computer and on
all my clothes.
I stormed upstairs to my mom's room.
My little brother peered out of his door.

"What's wrong?" He giggled, then slammed his door as hard as he could.
"MOM! YOUR SON PUT FUCKING HAM ALL OVER MY ROOM!" My little brother stood behind me, hysterically laughing.
"No, I didn't! She's crazy!"
The Big Bang Theory was on. She turned to me, molasses.
"Bella…"
"MOM!"
"What?"
"There's ham all over my room!"
"Can't you take a joke?! God!" Said my little brother.
My mom smiled. Slowly.
"Yeah, can't you take a joke?"
"I FUCKING HATE YOU!" I screamed, and I meant it.
"So, move out!" Yelled my little brother.
"Yeah, move out!" Echoed my mom.

I texted Jim back.
"Are you sure you don't want me to be there?"
Finally, he texted back one word:
"COME."

So I did. The house was blanketed in a thick, damp quiet. I found Jim atop his mattress on the floor beneath a Wonder Woman blanket, spooning Murdy who was breathing with maximum effort. Jim's eyes were puffy and he said nothing.

"Are you okay?"
"What kind of retarded fucking question is THAT?"
It was the wrong question. I sat on the floor at the foot of the bed, head hung, 18-years-old, doing my best to imitate someone who understood the gravity of loss.
Eventually a woman with wild red hair accompanied by a young Hispanic man entered with soothing, kind eyes. Jim sat up in bed.
 "Sweet, beautiful baby." Said the woman to Murdy. She rubbed his speckled belly, which rose and fell jaggedly. The Hispanic boy stood in the corner, gently smiling at the wall.

"Is this your father?" The woman asked
me.

"Yes." Jim responded before I had the
chance.

The woman slapped on plastic gloves
and removed a fat syringe full of viscus
fuchsia liquid from her kit.
"Shall we say a few words for Murdy?"
"No." Said Jim.

A graceful jab. The needle glugged into
Murdy's spine. Until that moment I had
been doing an impression of sadness. A
caricature. But now I was choking,
drowning, chest enclaving, body
disappearing, slipping away. I gasped
loudly. The kid and the woman looked at
me. Jim did not. I reached for Jim's
shoulder. He grabbed my hand tight.

Murdy began breathing faster and faster
and wagging his tail. He smiled up at
Jim "My boy. My boy." Jim whispered in
his ear. "My boy. My boy. My boy." The
room was swarmed by the smell of shit.

Murdy farted again and again. I threw up
in my mouth and swallowed it.
Murdy stopped moving. Jim closed
Murdy's eyes, then his own. He asked
us all to leave the room.

I offered the woman and the kid water or
tea, my voice cracking.
"Do you have anything stronger?" Asked
the woman, half joking. But I needed
something, too. I plucked some flower
from the bouquet hanging in Jim's closet
and the Hispanic kid rolled us a joint.
We sat in the living room and smoked,
the sound of Jim's wails and screams in
the background.

BLACK AND YELLOW BLACK AND
YELLOW BLACK AND YELLOW
BLACK AND YELLOW!

In Santa Barbara that same night, I
attended a party with the large assed
lover. I was underwater, still drowning. I
felt robbed of something I could not get
back. Girls my age in high top converse
twerked on walls and screamed the

words to Wiz Khalifa. I didn't feel anything like twerking which made me furious, furious with everyone adult who had sworn to keep me safe from this exact feeling and failed miserably. I hated Jim. I started working for him in search of stability but was exceedingly more traumatized now than when I started. I wanted to escape growing up, but working for Jim only expedited the process. Was there a person over 30 on this planet worth trusting? Any guiding voice that could stop the sinking? I could only recall my 4th grade teacher Miss McAdam.
"Today long division, tomorrow you're a grandma!"

The drowning overtook me. It bubbled out of my ass. I ran to the bathroom and shit my pants. There was no toilet paper and the flusher did not work.

BLACK AND YELLOW BLACK AND YELLOW BLACK AND YELLOW BLACK AND YELLOW!

I texted Jim from the bathroom, shit
trickling down my leg. "I love you but I
have to quit."
Eventually he wrote back "Love you 2.
Good idea."

3 years later, my Prius got repossessed
so I erected a GoFundMe campaign in
an attempt to raise the 1,500 dollars to
get it back from Big Toyota. I forwarded
the GoFundMe to every adult I knew,
including Jim.
"Isn't that for people with cancer?" Jim
asked via Facebook messenger.
"Haha, it's for people whose lives are
impacted by misfortune that are turning
to their communities for help."
"Go fuck yourself, bitch." He responded.
"You only talk to me when you want
something."

6 years after that, my mom passed
away. Photos of the two of them
splashed across his Facebook page.
"Fly free angel, the most beautiful
woman I have ever seen.
I will take care of them, I promise."

At the funeral he held me for what felt
like forever.
"My beautiful baby girl." He repeated
over and over, like a prayer. "My girl. My
girl. My girl." I remembered the day
Murdy died. "My boy. My boy. My boy."
he had whispered.
I was now the pitiful animal.

My fiancé stood behind me,
overzealous. He held out his hand. "I've
heard such great stories about you, Jim.
It's an honor."

Jim pivoted and walked away.

After the funeral, Jim was everywhere.
"My beautiful daughter, you take my
breath away." He commented on my
Instagram. "I'd love to take you and your
boyfriend out to dinner. Get a feel for
what he's all about. Don't forget, I am
your father."

I was starting to get angry.
"It's sweet." My older brother assured
me. "And he's lonely. What harm would
it do you to go to one dinner with him?"

"I'm 27 years old. I haven't even spoken to him in 9 years."
"So?"
"So, it's not fair for him to take credit for how I turned out. He barely knows me."
"Don't be selfish."
I kept pushing back the dinner. And rescheduling, and pushing back again.

I had come to understand that most adults over 55 have one shitty trip to the doctor then enter their "I'm dying" era. My mom would always say "You know my old friend Lisette…it's bad. They've given her 3 months to live…it's bad" and 3 months later Lisette would be at my house drinking 2 Buck Chuck with mom and smoking Camel Blues on the patio. My mom had this phase herself when I was in middle school. "Morgan, my time has come. Take care of your sister. I will watch over you — " she wrote in her journal. Then she lived, psychotically, for another 17 years.
So I didn't take it seriously when Jim entered *his* "I'm dying" era. Especially because…this was *Jim*.

Until that summer, when he went into in-
home hospice.
"I guess he was home on Friday and he
fell, then suddenly…his organs started
shutting down." My older brother, who
was out of town, explained.
"I think it's really important that you be
there with him."

I was back at Jim's, 11 years later. I
couldn't find his place at first. I
remembered it as the ugliest house on
the block, but seeing it now it was
actually beautiful. Exposed brick and
purple onion flowers. The inside seemed
so much smaller, especially because
they set Jim on a gurney bed in the
middle of the living room. He was under
the same Wonder Woman blanket
Murdy had died with.

Boomers came and boomers went,
paying respects. Writers, producers,
vaguely familiar Seinfeld era character
actors. They all had many demands of
me, most of them having something to
do with making the TV work. We sat

around for hours watching videos of Warren Zevon live.

Jim's skin suit, once boxy and puff chested, now lay lame and limp like a deflated pool float. His mouth was fully agape, brows raised. It was not unlike the face of someone cumming, which made sense because of the orgasmic amount of fentanyl keeping him comfortable. The rot from inside Jim enveloped the whole room in that hospital crusted warm aroma. I had to control my face from twisting in horror when I touched his cold milky skin, but I continued to stroke his arm out of fear I would regret it if I didn't.

Ginger showed up, an ex girlfriend with a binder of Jim's emails he had sent her over the years printed out for us all to read. I found this braggy and annoying, but quickly realized it was because I saw so much of myself in this woman, showing up at the death bed of an ex from 20 years ago, never ever having letting go. Not fully.

"I am so fucking taken by you I can't sleep." An email from jim5dogs@aol.com had written to Ginger in 2001. My now husband wrote me emails like this all the time and it hurt me, thinking about my husband and looking at Jim, thinking about the fact that I may see his body limp like a deflated pool float one day.

I read something recently (saw a TikTok) that said people only cry at weddings because they're thinking about their own shit. I think the same is true with death. Last year I had this foster dog for way too long, so long that I fell in love with her, and when she found a permanent home I was less heartbroken about her leaving and more heartbroken because of the guilt I felt toward myself for leaving her. She couldn't understand that I wasn't a bad person. I wasn't abandoning her. I realized now that maybe that's why Jim was so heartbroken over Murdy. Because he couldn't explain to Murdy what he meant to him.

And now I couldn't explain to Jim what he meant to me.

Which was, in many ways, everything. Still, I wasn't sad because he was dying. He was absolutely better off. He was the most miserable person I had ever met, and the loneliest, and I knew his soul wanted to be a kid again. Wanted that same stability I wanted when I showed up on his doorstep in my mom's kitten heels at 18-years-old. You could see it in every clay dip in every superhero foot he built; he wanted to make sturdy things with his kid brain. So I was certain he was off to be a baby in a family with a mother who made him feel safe. Maybe he'd be the kid of my pregnant social justice advocate neighbor Keegan, or Blake Lively's next kid, or maybe if God is feeling kooky, he'll be my kid someday.

I was really sad because in Jim's dying body, I saw that I too was getting older, that everything was moving, that if I closed my eyes and time traveled back to my 6th birthday, the adults I loved most and relied on most on this Earth were now off it. I felt alone. And I felt guilty for never letting Jim take Charlie

and I out to dinner. And for not rolling
with it when he called me his daughter.
Why not? In the end maybe we were
meant for each other, two Jews who
love dogs and have dirtbags for parents,
thinking they can hate themselves into
staying young forever. But I am strong
enough to revolt against that, and fall in
love with this planet again and again. To
be the only trustworthy person over 30.
Someone's gotta do it.

IMOGEN

The day I learned what romance was
Was the day he left me

Will you miss me? I asked him.
I knew you were gonna ask me that. I
will miss you but I won't miss this.

We sat in your Chevy at the end of the
cul de sac outside of Ed Bagley Jr.'s
house
And you held me as we listened
to Kissing You by Des'ree
your cashmere vanilla body
spray clawing at my throat
We decided we had to
get away from here Away from the boys
so desperate to dismember us
Hit Coinstar with your mom's mason jar
of change Cashed
in $22.57, put $15 in the tank
and we headed to Palm Springs
with a stolen bottle of cranberry Ciroc
We had $7.57 left to feed ourselves with
A feast of 7 McChickens!

We scraped resin out
of my crustiest pipe We took
Photo Booth pictures on the computer
I'd sneak away to call him from a
blocked number
and listen for girls in the background

You belong with Me by Taylor Swift
was the biggest song in the country
No matter how cute your baby is,
please don't forget the 7/11
on Palm Canyon Drive Shoving sleeves
of Ritz crackers down our pants
Higher than I knew was possible
Singing

*Dreaming bout the day when you wake
up and find that what you're looking for
has been here the whole time*

JESSICA

There were no sisters,
but there was my brother's girlfriend
Jessica
& for me there will always be Jessica
The only name in this book
I could never ever change

END

Rejoice, kitten! Silly
girl! Soon you will ache
for the
scab of

today!